Bethany Adams
Illustrated by Arnild C. Aldepolla
Return of the Elves
The Coloring Book  vol.1

# Soulbound

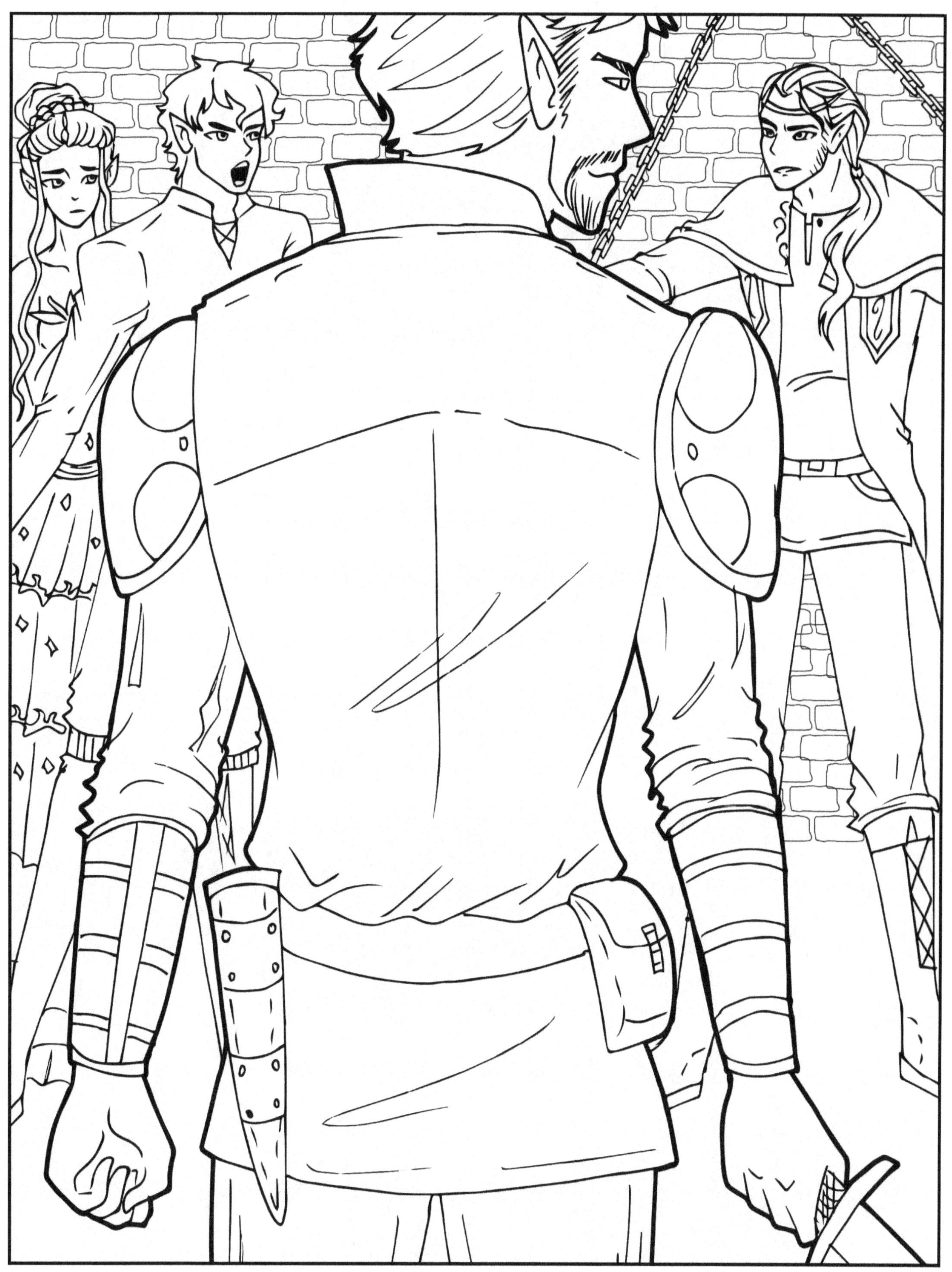

# Sundered

Exiled

# Seared

MAGIC TOUCH
MAGIC TOUCH
MAGIC TOUCH
CLOSED

Return
of the Elves

Don't Miss the Epic Series

Soulbound
Bethany Adams

Sundered
Bethany Adams

Exiled
Return of the Elves
Bethany Adams

Seared
Bethany Adams

www.ingramcontent.com/pod-product-compliance
Lightning Source LLC
Chambersburg PA
CBHW082103090726
47910CB00008B/2572